The LITTLE SCARECROW BOY

by MARGARET WISE BROWN Pictures by DAVID DIAZ

JOANNA COTLER BOOKS
An Imprint of HarperCollins Publishers

The display type is set in Petticoat and Ehmcke.

The text is set in Ehmcke.

The paintings in this book were created in watercolor, gouache,

and pencil on Arches watercolor paper.

Designed by David Diaz with special assistance from

Cecelia Zieba-Diaz and Julia Montroy.

The Little Scarecrow Boy

This edition copyright © 1998 by HarperCollins Publishers Inc.

Printed in the U.S.A. All rights reserved.

http://www.harperchildrens.com

Library of Congress Cataloging-in-Publication Data

Brown, Margaret Wise, 1910–1952.

    The little scarecrow boy / by Margaret Wise Brown ; illustrated by David Diaz.

    p.   cm.

    "Joanna Cotler Books."

    Summary: Early one morning, a little scarecrow whose father warns him that he is not fierce enough
to frighten a crow goes out into the cornfield alone.

    ISBN 0-06-026284-2. — ISBN 0-06-026290-7 (lib. bdg.)

    [1. Scarecrows—Fiction.   2. Fathers and sons—Fiction.]   I. Diaz, David, ill.   II. Title.

PZ7.B8163Ls 1998   97-32558

[E]—dc21   CIP

                                                            AC

1 2 3 4 5 6 7 8 9 10

❖

Newly illustrated edition

For my three precious children

who bring to my life joy

every day of the world.

— D.D.

ONCE UPON A TIME
in a cornfield there lived a scarecrow and his
scarecrow wife and their little scarecrow boy.

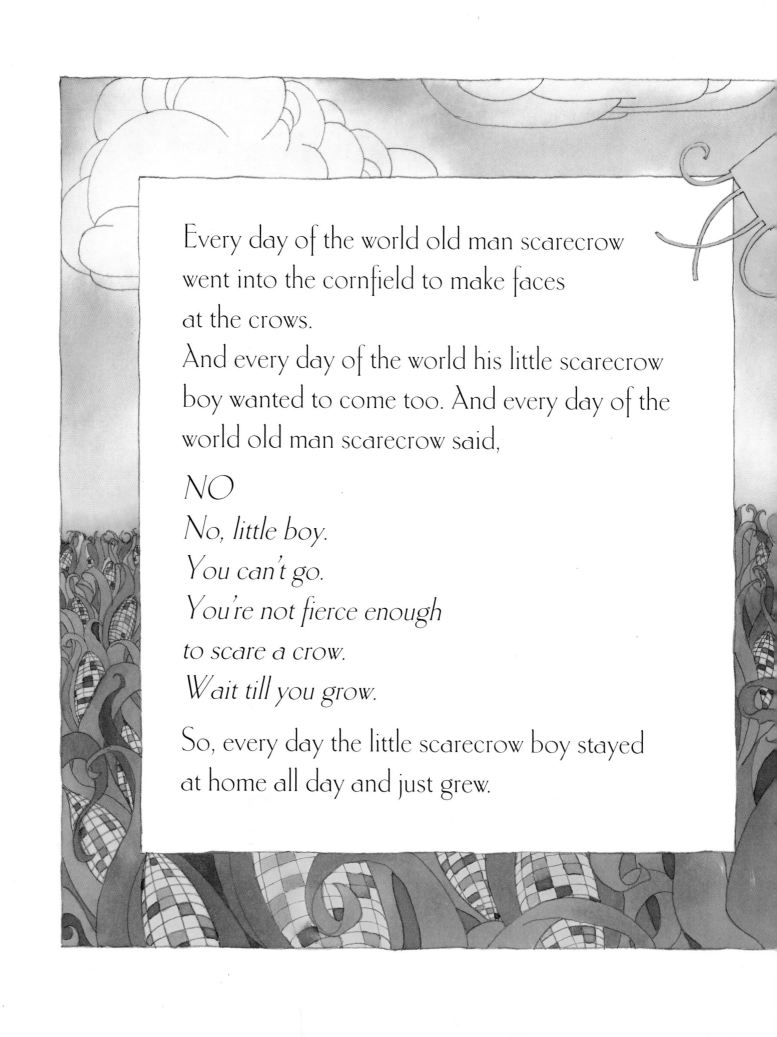

Every day of the world old man scarecrow
went into the cornfield to make faces
at the crows.
And every day of the world his little scarecrow
boy wanted to come too. And every day of the
world old man scarecrow said,

NO
No, little boy.
You can't go.
You're not fierce enough
to scare a crow.
Wait till you grow.

So, every day the little scarecrow boy stayed
at home all day and just grew.

Every day out in the field old man scarecrow waved his arms and made terrible faces. He made such terrible faces that the crows nearly lost their feathers at the sight of him there. And they flew far away, far away.

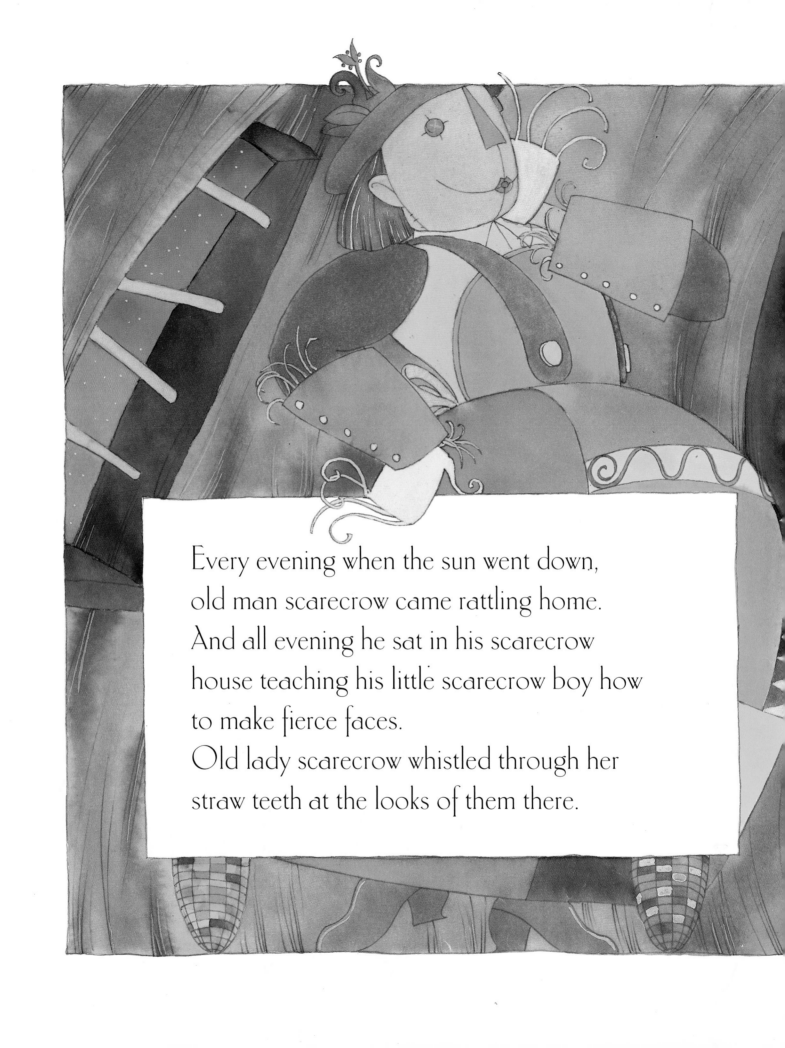

Every evening when the sun went down,
old man scarecrow came rattling home.
And all evening he sat in his scarecrow
house teaching his little scarecrow boy how
to make fierce faces.
Old lady scarecrow whistled through her
straw teeth at the looks of them there.

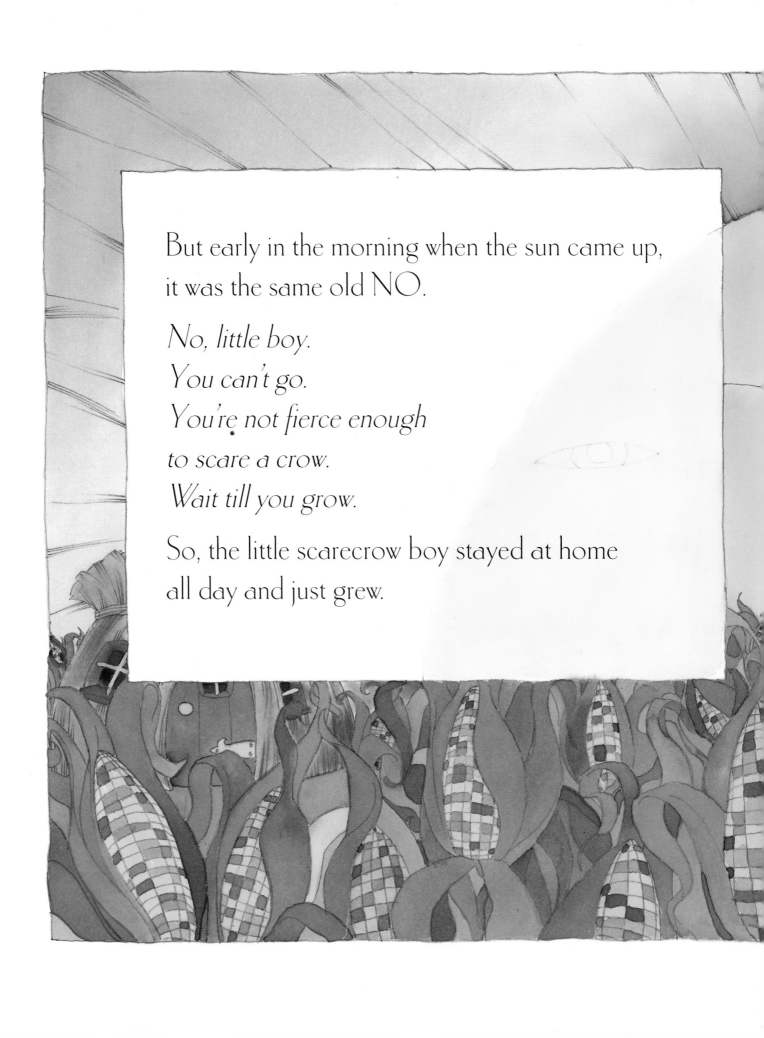

But early in the morning when the sun came up,
it was the same old NO.

No, little boy.
You can't go.
You're not fierce enough
to scare a crow.
Wait till you grow.

So, the little scarecrow boy stayed at home
all day and just grew.

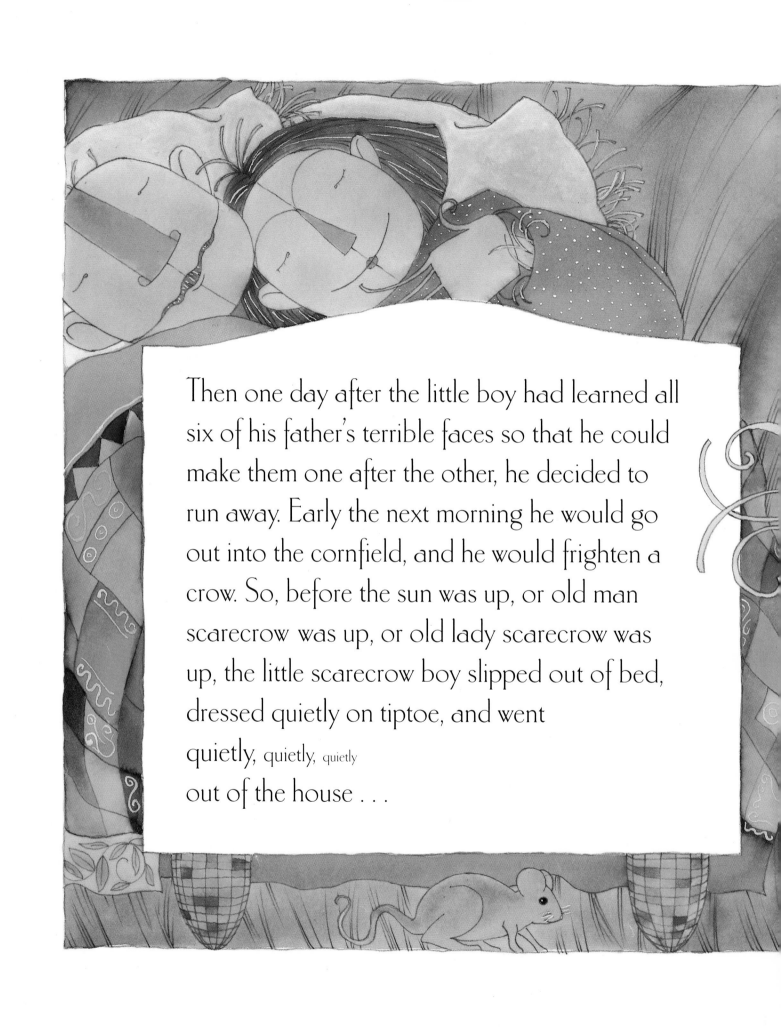

Then one day after the little boy had learned all
six of his father's terrible faces so that he could
make them one after the other, he decided to
run away. Early the next morning he would go
out into the cornfield, and he would frighten a
crow. So, before the sun was up, or old man
scarecrow was up, or old lady scarecrow was
up, the little scarecrow boy slipped out of bed,
dressed quietly on tiptoe, and went
quietly, quietly, quietly
out of the house . . .

. . . over to the cornfield
up on his father's post
in his father's place.

It was a fine shining morning with the sun
gleaming green down the corn blades.
Crows circled in the air far away over
the trees. The little scarecrow boy waved his
arms through the air. He had never felt fiercer
in all his life.
And then came flying a big black crow.

Oh Oh Oh

The little scarecrow made his first fierce face.
And still came flying the big black crow.

Oh Oh Oh
The little scarecrow boy made his
second fierce face.
And still came flying the big black crow.

His third face—

Oh Oh Oh

Time to go!—

So, the little scarecrow boy ran and he ran down the corn rows! The black flapping wings made a noise now, and looking back he could see the blue sky through the ragged feathers of the nearest crow.

He ran and he ran! Then he stopped.
His fourth face—
And still came flying the big black crow.
So, he ran and he ran and he ran and he ran.
And the crow flew and he flew and he flew
and he flew.
And the little scarecrow boy ran.

And then he made his fifth and next to fiercest
face of all!
And still came flying the big black crow!
The little boy had only one face left now and
hardly any breath. Even so, he stopped.
And with his arms stretched wide above his
head and his fingers drooping on
his hands he gave the big crow . . .

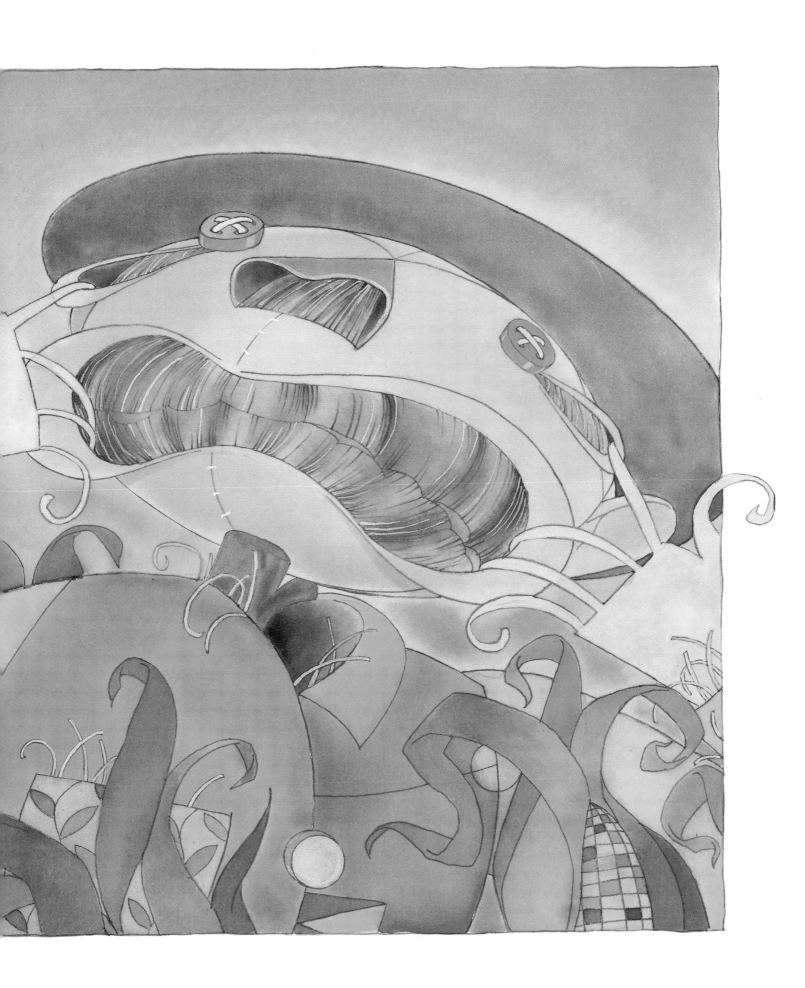

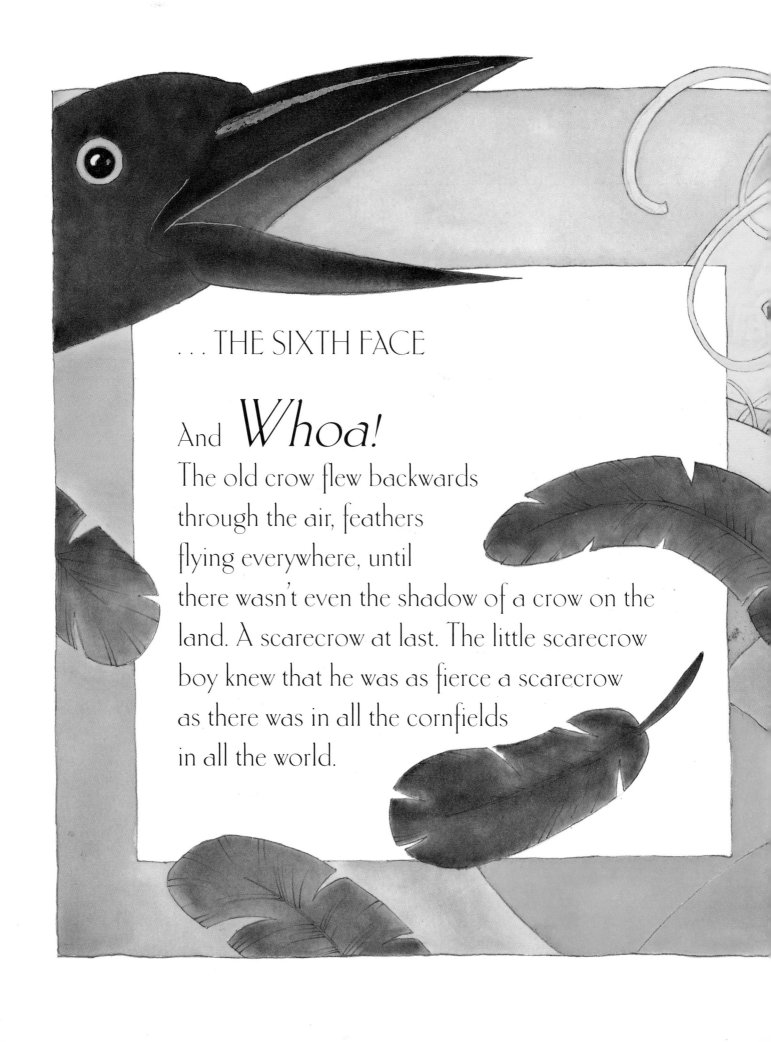

. . . THE SIXTH FACE

And *Whoa!*
The old crow flew backwards
through the air, feathers
flying everywhere, until
there wasn't even the shadow of a crow on the
land. A scarecrow at last. The little scarecrow
boy knew that he was as fierce a scarecrow
as there was in all the cornfields
in all the world.

And then he saw a shadow in front of him,
and he looked up, and there behind him was
old man scarecrow, his father.
And his father was proud of his little boy who
had made all six faces at the crows.

And he picked up his little scarecrow boy
in his scarecrow arms and they went home
to breakfast.

And when the little scarecrow grew up
he was the fiercest scarecrow in all the fields
in all the world.